A Frog Named Earl

– A Tale of Adventure, Courage, Friendship and Acceptance –

by

E. Trewin & S. Beyer

Just because you don't, doesn't mean you can't.

There once was a frog named Earl. Although Earl loved croaking at the moon, fly catching and playing tag with his friends, Earl did not get around the same way they did. You see, Earl is a frog that does not jump.

So instead of leaping from lily pad to lily pad on his own back legs, Earl used a solar powered pogo stick.

One day after a game of tag, Earl and his friends sat around a campfire as the older frogs told stories. One of the stories told was about a wise old owl named Owen who lived in a giant oak tree at the end of the spring rainbow. He was known to help all creatures overcome any problems or challenges no matter how big or how small.

Lying in bed that night, Earl could not stop thinking of Owen. The story interested him because he had always dreamed of playing at the pond with his friends using his own back legs to hop around, rather than relying on his pogo stick.

Early the next morning, Earl stuffed his backpack with some tasty fly sandwiches, and set out to find Owen, the wise old owl.

Earl hadn't gone far before he came across a tall fence, at least four feet high, which crossed the path he was traveling. Now, for most frogs, this fence would have been much too high to leap over, but not for Earl.

With one mighty bounce, Earl and his pogo stick easily cleared the fence and he continued on his journey.

Earl moved along steadily on this warm sunny day. Soon, he found himself at the foot of a rushing river. Since this was the first time Earl had been so far from his pond, he had never seen so much water before.

The river was much too wide even for Earl's trusty pogo stick to leap across. Looking up and down the river, Earl could not see a bridge or any other way to help him cross to the other side. After exploring for a while, Earl lost hope and sadly decided to turn around and head back home.

At just that moment, Earl heard a swishing sound coming from the water. When he turned to see what was making the noise, Earl saw something quite astonishing. It was a small red fish, wearing a baseball cap... in a rowboat!

Seeing Earl standing by the riverbank, the small fish rowed over and introduced himself.

"Hello Mr. frog, my name is Zander," said the friendly fish.

Zander explained to Earl that he was a fish that did not swim. Instead, he used a rowboat to travel up and down the river. As the two spoke, Earl told Zander all about Owen and his quest to find the wise old owl.

After hearing about Earl's plan, Zander offered him a ride across the river and asked if he could join him on his journey. You see, as much as he loved his little boat, Zander had always wanted to swim on his own like all the other fish in his school. He hoped that Owen would be able to help him as well.

A few minutes later, Earl, his pogo stick, and Zander were making their way across the river in the tiny rowboat.

Once across the river, Earl secured Zander and his fishbowl in his backpack, got on his pogo stick, and the two new friends were on their way.

After avoiding several obstacles with some nifty pogo sticking by Earl, the duo came upon and entered a tall forest. The two were enjoying themselves, when suddenly Earl's pogo stick hit a rock. The sudden jolt caused Zander to soar out of Earl's backpack and land gently on a nearby tree limb.

Now, Earl and Zander found themselves in quite a pickle.

Although Earl could easily bounce high enough to reach Zander, he was unable to grab the fishbowl while holding on to the pogo stick handles. Zander was surely stuck alright, and there was no way for Earl to help his new friend.

While Earl sat under the tree pondering the situation, he looked up and saw a monkey skipping towards them, and she was carrying a ladder under her arm.

"Hi, my name is Carli," said the perky Monkey. "What's going on here?"

"My friend is stuck in this tree, and I can't get him down," Earl replied.

"Oh, that's all?" Carli asked. With no hesitation, Carli grabbed her ladder, placed it against the tree and shimmied up. In a flash, Carli was back down the ladder holding Zander and the fishbowl in her arms.

Zander thanked the kind monkey for her help and asked why she happened to be carrying a ladder through the forest. Carli explained that she is a monkey that does not climb trees. Instead, she uses her ladder to go up trees whenever she wants to gather bananas or play with her monkey friends.

It was now lunchtime, so they decided to sit under the tree to eat. Earl shared one of his fly sandwiches with Zander (which just happened to be one of his favorites), while Carli ate a tasty banana.

By the time they were finished eating, it was decided that Carli would join Earl and Zander on their quest to find Owen. Carli had always wondered what it would be like to climb trees like the other monkeys in the forest. She hoped that Owen would be able to help her as well.

It wasn't long before they were all on their way. And that's how two friends became three.

The new friends finally found their way out of the forest and made their way to a green meadow. It was there that they saw a beautiful rainbow in the distance. Earl remembered hearing of the rainbow during the campfire stories, and he instantly knew they were nearing the home of Owen, the wise old owl.

With hopeful excitement, the three new friends increased their pace. Earl on his pogo stick, Zander safely secured in his backpack, and Carli skipping swiftly by their side.

As they continued on their journey and looked ahead, they slowed and came to a stop. Directly in front of them was an unexpected obstacle. Sitting between them and the rainbow was a huge canyon that looked to be a mile deep and twice as wide. Their hearts sank.

On the other side of the canyon, they could see a gigantic oak tree that stood alone at the end of the rainbow. The tree was surely the home of Owen, the wise old owl.

The trio stood by the edge of the canyon, feeling dejected. They knew there was no way for them to cross the canyon to meet Owen. Sadly, it seemed like their journey was about to come to an end once again.

Just as they were about to end their quest, Carli looked up and saw the most amazing sight. It was a red robin... in the basket of a hot air balloon.

Noticing the travelers, the colorful and friendly robin expertly landed her balloon next to Earl, Zander and Carli and introduced herself.

"Hello, my name is Rae Rae," said the robin, who did not fly like other birds.

Instead, she traveled the skies in her hot air balloon. Being a curious bird, she asked how it was that they found themselves at the edge of the canyon, so far from a pond, a river, or a forest.

Earl, Zander and Carli took turns telling their part of the day's events and their quest to find Owen. When they were finished telling their story, Rae Rae offered to take them across the canyon in her hot air balloon. In return, Rae Rae asked if she could join them to meet Owen. She had always wanted to fly high in the clouds using her own two wings rather than relying on her balloon.

They all happily agreed, and in no time at all they were soaring high in the sky floating effortlessly towards their destination.

And that is how three friends became four.

Shortly after landing on the other side of the canyon, the four friends were greeted by a horse… on roller skates! The horse skated over and introduced himself as Noah.

"Cool hot air balloon!" said Noah in a horsey voice.

"Thanks, your wheels are pretty cool too," Rae Rae replied. "I've never seen a horse on roller skates."

Noah smiled and explained how he never learned to trot like the rest of his horse buddies. Instead, he uses his roller skates to travel the countryside.

"Do you know where to find Owen, the wise old owl?" Earl asked.

"I sure do!" said Noah. "I can escort you to him if you'd like."

They all agreed and followed Noah as he skated swiftly toward the large oak tree they had seen earlier. When they got to the foot of the tree, they peered and saw a magnificent owl wearing dark sunglasses. They had finally found Owen, the wise old owl.

"Hello, *whooo's* there?" the old owl hooted as they approached.

"Hi, I'm Earl, and these are my friends, Zander, Carli and Rae Rae. Are you Owen, the wise old owl?" said the frog.

"Well, my name is Owen, that is true. I suppose it is a matter of opinion as to how wise I am," he chuckled. "How may I be of service?" he asked.

Earl proceeded to tell Owen all about their journey. He told Owen how he and his friends had traveled so far to meet him, and how they hoped that with all his wisdom, Owen might be able to help them overcome their personal challenges. Earl further explained how he and his friends wished they could do the same things other frogs, fish, monkeys and birds do.

After listening carefully, Owen cleared his throat and began to speak.

"It sounds like the four of you have had quite an adventurous and memorable day."

"This old tree has been my home for many years," Owen continued. "Do you know this is the first time a frog, a fish or a monkey has ever crossed from the other side of the canyon? That is a remarkable accomplishment."

"Yes, you may face challenges that others do not, but keep in mind that it is because of those challenges and not in spite of them that you were able to make this successful journey. Throughout this day, you have made new friends, accepted each other for who you are, and used each other's special talents to come this far."

Owen hesitated then continued, "You may not know this but I am blind," he said, "but sometimes I believe I can see more clearly than those with perfect vision."

"What I can see is how Earl was able to help Zander travel through the forest on his pogo stick. Zander was able to help Earl across a rushing river, and if it hadn't been for Carli, Zander might still be stuck in that tree. And keep in mind that your journey would have surely ended at the edge of the canyon had Rae Rae not come along in her hot air balloon to help three strangers.

"Not bad for a frog that does not jump, a fish that does not swim, a monkey that does not climb and a robin that does not fly," he concluded.

...Owen was truly a wise old owl!!!

The four new friends knew that everything Owen said was true. They looked at each other with huge smiles and felt a new appreciation for the journey they had just made and with whom they made it.

Full of confidence and hope for the future, they thanked Owen before heading back to their homes. Rae Rae volunteered to give them all a ride in her hot air balloon... because that is what friends do!

After she delivered Carli to the end of the forest, Zander to his rowboat at the riverbank, and Earl safely to his pond, Rae Rae effortlessly turned her hot air balloon around and returned home.

So, what ever happened to our new friends?

Carli decided to open an ice cream stand in the forest. Her best-selling ice cream is, of course, made of fresh bananas... which she insists on gathering herself.

For the next few years, Zander decided to take his rowboat to many new places. He began new adventures and met all sorts of new characters. Often telling the story of his unforgettable journey to see a wise old owl.

Rae Rae continued to travel the countryside, but not by herself. She met up and was accompanied by Noah, the friendly horse she met on the other side of the canyon. So, if you happen to see a robin in a hot air balloon and a horse roller skating swiftly beneath her, chances are it is them.

As for Earl. Well, Earl was greeted by his friend Lisa when he came back from his adventure. They were married a few years later! Zander, Carli, Rae Rae, Noah and Owen all attended the happy wedding.

28

The End... for now.

Made in United States
North Haven, CT
26 July 2022

21876061R00022